The Tale of Squirrel Nutkin

A Story about Being Polite

Retold by Sarah Albee
Illustrated by Jill Bauman

Famous Fables ™

Reader's Digest Young Families

This is a tale about a tail—a little red squirrel's tail. The little red squirrel's name was Nutkin. He had one brother, named Twinkleberry, and many cousins. All the squirrels lived in the forest by a lake. And in the middle of the lake was a lovely island covered with nut trees.

One autumn day, Nutkin and Twinkleberry and the other squirrels decided to go to the island and gather nuts for the coming winter. The squirrels made little rafts from twigs, and oars from fallen branches. Then they spread out their tails and used them for sails.

Each squirrel carried a small sack to hold the nuts he was going to gather. The polite squirrels also brought some berries to give to Old Mr. Brown, the owl who lived in a hollow oak tree and watched over the island.

Each squirrel in turn bowed to the owl. Twinkleberry asked, "Old Mr. Brown, would you be so kind as to allow us to gather nuts on your island?"

But Nutkin did not bow. He did not have good manners. He waved his big bushy tail and began singing this riddle—

"I have four nuts and you have none.
If I give you three, I'll have just…"

The owl paid no attention.

The busy squirrels spent the day filling their sacks with nuts. Then they sailed away, tired and hungry.

The next morning, the squirrels went back to the island. This time they brought some crab apples as a gift for Old Mr. Brown.

Twinkleberry said, "Old Mr. Brown, will you please be so kind as to let us gather more nuts today?"

But Nutkin danced up and down, tickling the old owl with a thorny branch, singing—

"Old Mr. Brown. How rumply you are!
Can you spell that without an R?"

Once again, Old Mr. Brown paid no attention to Nutkin. He gathered up his apples and went into his home inside the oak tree.

Twinkleberry and the other little squirrels filled their sacks with golden nuts, getting ready for the cold months ahead. But Nutkin did not put any nuts into his sack. Instead, he laid them on a tree stump and played marbles with them all day long.

On the third day, the squirrels got up very early. They went fishing and caught seven fat minnows. The squirrels paddled over the lake and gave their minnows to Old Mr. Brown. All except Nutkin.

How many minnows did Nutkin bring? None! That naughty little squirrel poked Old Mr. Brown, singing—
"Here is a riddle. Can you tell me:
How many strawberries grow in the sea?
Of course you can't, for I'm sure you
don't know.
It's as many goldfish as swim in the snow!"

Old Mr. Brown collected his minnows and took no interest in Nutkin or his rude little riddle.

On the fourth day, the squirrels brought Old Mr. Brown a present of wild honey. It was sweet and sticky.

But Nutkin had not helped to gather the honey. Instead, he skipped up and down, and sang—

> "*Buzz-buzz-buzz says the little yellow bee!*
> *What have those squirrels taken from me?*"

Old Mr. Brown rolled his eyes at Nutkin's rudeness and picked up his jar of honey.

Nutkin should have left well enough alone, but he didn't. He danced and he pranced, waved his big bushy tail to and fro and shouted—

"Skiperdee-doodle!
You're soft in the noodle!
Old Mr. Brown,
You'd better leave town!"

Foolish Nutkin grew bolder!

"Old Mr. Brown!
Get out of town!
Fly, I say!
Fly far, far away!"

And still Old Mr. Brown said nothing at all.

Nutkin laughed at the owl. Then he ran straight at Old Mr. Brown and jumped right on top of his head!

All at once there was a flutter and a scuffle and one loud "Squeak!"

The other squirrels scampered into the bushes as fast as they could.

When they came out again, they saw Old Mr. Brown standing quite still—as if nothing at all had happened.

But there was Nutkin, being held upside-down by his tail! The wise old owl had caught the rude squirrel. Was this to be the end of Squirrel Nutkin?

Old Mr. Brown carried Nutkin, who was now quite afraid, into his house. The owl held the squirrel tightly, but Nutkin pulled so hard on his own tail that it broke in two! He dashed up the stairs and escaped out the attic window.

And to this day, if you meet Nutkin, don't ask him for a riddle. But if you do, this very naughty little squirrel may still shout and stamp his feet. But he surely won't be waving a big bushy tail!

Famous Fables, Lasting Virtues
Tips for Parents

Now that you've read The Tale of Squirrel Nutkin, *use these pages as a guide to teach your child the virtues in the story. By talking about the story and its message and engaging in the suggested activities, you can help your child develop good judgment and a strong moral character.*

About Being Polite

Very young children are naturally curious about everything around them, including people they see in public. But sometimes young children point out what they see in a loud voice, such as, "Mommy, look! That man has no hair!" Almost all parents have had the experience of being embarrassed when their child makes an inappropriate remark like this one. Usually, we make our apologies and then leave the scene as quickly as we can. How can we teach our children to be polite without squelching their natural curiosity and keen observation skills? Here are some strategies:

1. *Rehearse in advance.* Before you leave for a shopping mall, or preschool, or a big family event like a wedding, stage a dress rehearsal. Review with your children what behavior you expect of them. Practice with them by pretending you are a salesperson or another shopper or a teacher. Use props to help demonstrate your ideas about what is appropriate to say or do in public and what is not.

2. *Take a positive approach.* Rather than saying, "Don't talk in such a loud voice," say, "Please use a quieter voice." Teach your child that he can tell you what he is thinking about someone else by whispering in your ear or by waiting until the two of you are in a more private place.

3. *Be realistic.* It is important to have age-appropriate expectations for our children. Inappropriate behavior often occurs when children are tired or hungry. Make every effort to be sure they have had adequate rest and nutritious food before taking them on an outing. For a positive outcome, try to balance the length of the outing with their energy level.